THE DARK OF KNIGHT

By
Charlotte Fullerton

SCHOLASTIC INC.

NEW YORK TORONTO LONDON AUCKLAND
SYDNEY MEXICO CITY NEW DELHI HONG KONG

No part of this work may be reproduced in whole or in part, or stored in a retrieval system, or transmitted in any form or by any means, electronic, mechanical, photocopying, recording, or otherwise, without written permission of the publisher. For information regarding permission, write to Scholastic Inc., Attention: Permissions Department, 557 Broadway, New York, NY 10012.

ISBN: 978-0-545-20627-3

Cartoon Network, the logo, BEN 10 ALIEN FORCE and all related characters and elements are trademarks of and © 2010 Cartoon Network.
Published by Scholastic Inc.
SCHOLASTIC and associated logos are trademarks and/or registered trademarks of Scholastic Inc.

12 11 10 9 8 7 6 5 4 3 2 1   10 11 12 13 14 15/0

Designed by Rick DeMonico
Printed in the U.S.A.   40
First printing, April 2010

CHAPTER ONE

O n your left, Tennyson!"

Kevin Levin's cool, raspy voice echoed over the deafening barrage of laser fire coming at him from every direction.

At night, warehouses by the shady docks in any city would be considered dangerous. But the current attack was way above and beyond what any normal town would expect. Then again, Bellwood was hardly a normal town.

"Ha!" Kevin leaped through the air, grunting with effort. As he did, his fist grew, stretched, and morphed into a giant boulder. With a resounding *gong*, it struck the knight in shining armor who was charging at his friend.

The Forever Knight—as these medieval-looking villains were known—wobbled in place for a moment. He held onto his helmeted head as his whole body vibrated like a bell. Then he collapsed to the ground in a clanging heap.

"I saw him, Kevin! Chill, will you?" Big Chill called back in his usual breathy voice.

The thin, blue, bug-eyed alien unfurled his hooded cloak into a pair of bisected wings and zoomed straight up into the air as two more Forever Knights tried to close in on him from either side.

A member of the alien species known as a Necrofriggian ("necro" meaning death and "frigid" meaning extremely cold), native to a subzero planet called Kylmyys, Big Chill was so named by Ben because he had the mysterious ability to freeze objects with his breath or touch—and that is precisely what the creature did now. Hovering above his would-be attackers, Big Chill exhaled a gust of freezing wind, covering the knights' armor in a sheet of ice that pinned their arms to their sides and their feet to the ground.

"Forsooth!" exclaimed one of the knights as he toppled over. The other's teeth were too busy chattering to say anything.

"Hold it right there, you two," breathed Big Chill. "I mean, *freeze*! Heh heh."

Every time Ben took this particular alien form, he couldn't resist making puns that referenced the low temperature.

"Cool it with the cold jokes, will you, Ben?" Gwen Tennyson sighed at her cousin. She was busy using her own alien-enhanced abilities to generate powerful magenta shields of pure energy to protect herself from the zigzagging red blasts that tore through the air. The remaining Forever Knights had not slowed down their attack.

"Heh. You said 'cool it,'" chuckled Big Chill, his cloud of icy breath visible in the still night air.

"Why did you turn into Big Chill, anyway?" asked Kevin with more than a hint of irritation. He was struggling to fight off some Forever Knights in hand-to-hand combat. Or in Kevin's case, hand-to-giant-rock-fist combat. "I mean, come on!" he continued. "The Forever Knights wear armor, dude. That's metal. Lodestar could've taken these guys out with one, uh, magnet tied behind his back!"

"Don't you think I tried to turn into Lodestar, Kevin?" asked Big Chill, making himself intangible just in time to allow several laser blasts to pass harmlessly through him.

The Omnitrix was malfunctioning a lot these days. Much as Ben hated to admit it, it was largely his own fault. The Omnitrix was the single most powerful device in the entire universe, and fifteen-year-old Ben Tennyson held the awesome responsibility of wielding it wisely. Some days he lived up to this responsibility better than others.

Created by a tiny, gray, froglike alien named Azmuth of the Galvan—the most brilliant mind the universe had ever known—the Omnitrix was an amazing genetic-manipulating device the size and shape of a wristwatch. It had arrived on Earth in grave distress five years ago, seeking the only being in the galaxy worthy to bear it: Ben and Gwen's paternal grandfather, Max Tennyson.

Back in those days, ten-year-old Ben and Gwen had no idea their Grandpa Max was part of a super-secret intergalactic law enforcement organization called the Plumbers, who were charged with the task of monitoring all extra-terrestrial activity and keeping peace both on Earth and in space. In fact, Max was the Plumbers' most honorable, decorated, skilled, and important member.

That's why the imperiled Omnitrix had sought him by coming to Earth.

However, it was ten-year-old Ben who had stumbled upon the incredible alien device during a summer camping trip with his grandpa and Gwen. Because he was related to Grandpa Max, Ben's DNA was a close enough genetic match to the human being the Omnitrix was actually seeking. On that fateful night, the powerful, one-of-a-kind contraption latched onto Ben's wrist instead of his grandfather's. And it would not come off.

Ever since then — with the notable exception of a five-year hiatus during which he was free from the device — Ben had used the Omnitrix to turn himself into a vast array of strange and powerful alien life forms.

Access to these creatures had originally been unlocked ten at a time — for simplicity's sake in cataloging them, according to Azmuth. Though the Omnitrix's creator had told Ben that a total of 1,000,903 genetic samples were theoretically available, and the Omnitrix had the capability of sampling many more.

Ben had gradually learned how to use each of his alien forms to fight super-powered evildoers of both human and alien origin, to protect the innocent, and even to defend the whole Earth itself from an all-out invasion by a supremacist species called the HighBreed. It had taken him a while—five years, to be exact—but Ben had finally stepped up and realized what it meant to be a hero. He'd even earned the respect of the Omnitrix's temperamental inventor.

Until he and his former bitter enemy, now dependable ally, Kevin Levin, had attempted to hack the Omnitrix to gain access to even more of the watch's power. Their plan had backfired, and the surge of energy they'd released had tampered with forces beyond their control. They'd damaged the Omnitrix and rendered many of its functions unpredictable. Now, no matter which alien he chose, Ben could never be sure what he was going to turn into.

But Kevin's predicament was even worse. The powerful genetic energy the Omnitrix had unleashed had mutated Kevin. Instead of being able to absorb materials onto his human body, Kevin was actually made up of a mishmash of different materials—permanently.

Kevin's powers had changed, too. Instead of flesh, Kevin was now made of stone, metal, and various other materials. He could turn his fists into boulders, anvils, mallets, or other simple tools that would be useful in a fight. Though his hands could return to their basic human shape, they, along with his arms, legs, torso, and his face remained altered by the hodgepodge of inhuman materials he was made of.

In order to hide his new form, Kevin wore an ID mask that restored his former human appearance. Even though deep down he knew that his state was at least partially his own fault, Kevin put the blame for his misery squarely on one person: Ben.

"So you tried to turn into Lodestar. Do I look like I care?" Kevin growled at Big Chill, hammering Forever Knights out of his way with his huge metallic fists.

"You're the one who asked," Big Chill breathed back, equally irritated. Ben knew perfectly well that if the Omnitrix had just turned him into his Lodestar, like he'd wanted, this fight would have been over almost immediately. He didn't need Kevin to rub it in.

"What are these Forever Knights doing anyway?" Gwen's voice rang out above the din of the laser fire as she blasted Forever Knights with magenta energy beams.

"What are they always doing?" Kevin barked. "Probably stealing alien tech. Duh!"

He immediately regretted his tone of voice. Kevin knew it wasn't right to take out his frustration on Gwen.

She didn't have anything to do with the accident that had disfigured him. And she hadn't been anything but loving and supportive toward him, despite how repulsive he knew he must be to her now. How could Gwen possibly want to be his girlfriend now that he looked like this? He was sure it was only a matter of time before she dumped him. Who wouldn't? Kevin angrily punched an unlucky Forever Knight with his anvil hand.

The thought of dumping Kevin had never crossed Gwen's mind. In fact, in her every spare waking moment, Gwen was working hard to try to figure out a cure for Kevin's monstrous disfiguration. She had even gone back to using her old book of magic spells as a possible means to discover a solution. She was determined to come up with some way—any way—to help Kevin.

"I know the Forever Knights are usually at the docks trying to steal alien tech," Gwen retorted huffily. "What I meant was, what are they doing with *that*?"

Two of the remaining Forever Knights were trying to sneak away with a wooden crate. Gwen lassoed them with a ropelike beam of manna and jerked the heavily armored bad guys together, crushing the wooden box between them into splinters. The knights struggled helplessly, bound by Gwen's powerful energy stream, as a strange alien artifact fell to the ground at their feet.

"And don't 'duh' me," Gwen finished, turning to glare at Kevin.

"Sorry," Kevin apologized.

"Allow me," Big Chill breathed in his creepy voice, swooping in to grab the piece of alien handiwork. His semitransparent, ghostlike self passed right through the cluster of knights, but Big Chill had to make himself tangible to pick up the object from the ground.

"Ah!" Big Chill cried out as soon as his fingers made contact with the strange alien artifact. A blinding flash of green light engulfed him, forcibly transforming him back into Ben Tennyson!

Ben crumpled to the ground with a groan.

Ben!" cried Gwen, rushing to her cousin's side.

Kevin swung around and batted away the remaining Forever Knights with the huge iron ball that was his fist.

"What happened?" murmured Ben groggily. One second he'd been Big Chill, the next he was his regular human self, all without ever activating the Omnitrix. That wasn't the way the watch usually worked.

"Must have been that alien artifact," Gwen said, pointing to the mysterious object on the ground beside Ben. If it was powerful enough to affect Ben like that, they'd better not leave the thing lying around.

"Ah!" she shrieked, dropping the piece of strange material like it was a hot potato. "It burns!"

As soon as Gwen touched the artifact, all the magenta energy still lingering on the scene instantly dissolved. As her manna lasso faded away from the group of Forever Knights, they took the opportunity to escape.

"Run away! Run away!" they cried.

Kevin saw them go, but he had more important things on his mind. He rushed to Gwen's side. "You okay?"

"I-I think so," she stammered, rubbing her hand where it had touched the device.

"It must be some kind of energy conduit," added Ben, shaking his head to clear it. He got to his feet. "Never seen anything like it before."

"Wonder if my old running buddy Argit and I could get a good price for it on the black market," mused Kevin. Kevin and his untrustworthy alien pal Argit had been involved in many a shady business dealing together in the past, including boosting Grandpa Max's old camper, the Rustbucket. Argit and Kevin had conspired to sell off the myriad alien tech Grandpa Max had installed in the Rustbucket. That plan had not gone very well for Kevin. He still didn't like talking about it.

Belatedly, Kevin noticed that Ben and Gwen were staring at him with displeasure. "I meant 'we.' Maybe *we* could get a good price for it. I was going to share with you guys," Kevin covered.

"Uh-huh," Ben frowned, somewhat suspiciously. After all the adventures they'd been through together, Ben had grown to trust Kevin, often with his own life. But occasionally there were little moments like these, when Kevin would let a hint of his old self slip out. Ben couldn't help wondering if their so-called "friend" Kevin was always one hundred percent reliable.

"Stand back," Ben said. "This could get ugly."

He took off his long-sleeved green jacket with white racing stripes and a black-and-white "10" and wadded it up over his hand protectively as he reached for the alien artifact.

"Ugly's my middle name now," said Kevin, brushing Ben's cloth-covered hand aside.

"I thought your middle name was Ethan," smiled Gwen. She elbowed him in a good-natured way. "Kevin E. Levin. Somebody's parents had a sense of humor." She giggled.

"Right, *Gwen*. And *Ben*. And what's your brother's

name again? Oh, that's right: *Ken!*" Kevin smirked back. "I'm just surprised Grandpa Max's name isn't *Glen*."

"Now, now, kids," said Ben, stepping in between his friends like a referee. "Don't make me separate you two."

"Seriously, though," Kevin interjected, the smile dropping from his face. "I think I've heard of this kind of alien tech. But I never believed it was real."

Kevin squinted down at the piece. At first glance, it appeared to be an ordinary hunk of rock, but upon closer inspection, it was revealed to be a foreign metallic compound of a sort not found on Earth. Etched into its surface were strange markings, alien glyphs, which the well-traveled Kevin now strained to decipher.

"Can you make out what it says?" Gwen asked him.

Kevin had surprised his friends several times in the past with his ability to read alien languages. For a guy without much formal schooling, Kevin was actually pretty knowledgeable — especially about matters of alien significance.

But as he studied the particular alien object before him now, Kevin frowned and tipped his head to the side. "It's only got pieces of letters on it, I think, no whole words," he said.

The alien artifact had jagged edges. It looked as if it had been chipped off a much larger object, almost like a single piece of a larger puzzle.

"Whatever it is, we'd better not leave it here," Ben said grimly. "It's obviously pretty powerful, and the Forever Knights are bound to come back for it."

Ben reached for the artifact again, but Kevin intercepted the move with his own inhuman palm.

"You've both got energy powers," Kevin said, nodding toward Ben and Gwen. "I don't. Not anymore." He hung his head in sadness for just a moment, then looked up. "Let me have a crack at it."

Ben and Gwen stood by tensely, prepared to intervene at a moment's notice if necessary to rescue their friend from any ill effects of the artifact. After what it had done to each of them, who knew what it might do to Kevin?

Kevin wiggled his fingers in the air above the piece, hesitated for a beat, then grabbed it.

Everybody winced in anticipation. But nothing happened.

"Huh," Kevin grunted, surprised and a little disappointed.

"Must have used up all its power on us," Ben ventured a guess.

"Maybe," said Gwen, not at all convinced.

"I wonder what the Forever Knights were going to do with it?" Ben wondered aloud.

"Doesn't matter now." Kevin tossed the seemingly inert artifact up in the air a couple of times with satisfaction. "Finders' keepers. Losers," he paused, then shrugged, "losers."

CHAPTER THREE

Meanwhile, inside a massive gray stone fortress on a lonely hillside, dozens of Forever Knights were assembled like soldiers in formation, facing an impressively adorned altar at the far end of a gothic chamber. Like the knights Ben, Gwen, and Kevin had just encountered, they all wore suits of full-plate, medieval armor, with helmets and visors obscuring their identities. A sideways number "8"—the infinity symbol—was emblazoned prominently on the midsection of each suit of armor. This was the hallowed insignia of the brotherhood of the Forever Knights.

Enormous ornate stained glass windows lined the great hall. Their elaborate, semi-opaque pictures told grand, sweeping tales of the Order's many deeds of chivalry and heroism throughout the ages. Or at least, the knights believed those deeds had been chivalrous and heroic. Others may have disagreed—strongly.

Among their many instances of infamy, the Forever Knights had recently been in the business of trading for alien tech with the DNAliens, a mysterious and extremely numerous race of frightening plant-based creatures with grotesque exposed brains and a propensity for spitting sticky resin at their prey. As it turned out, these DNAliens were actually part human—captive Earthlings mutated and enslaved by an invading alien species called the HighBreed. It was only thanks to Ben Tennyson and his team of friends that the HighBreed invasion had failed. That the Forever Knights would be in league with such villains spoke volumes about them.

Several grand medieval tapestries hung from the walls of the great hall, covering them from floor to ceiling. These depicted the exciting exploits of knights in shining armor versus the terrible fire-breathing dragon they had been honor-bound to contain for centuries. It was because of this very creature that myths about the existence of dragons sprang up in the first place.

After a thousand years of captivity under the

dutiful watch of the Forever Knights, this very dragon had actually turned out to be an alien creature from outer space, held against his will through no fault of his own.

The Forever Knights weren't known for their brains. But they were heavily armed, numerous, organized, and motivated. All they ever required was strong leadership and a noble task to be set upon.

"So say we?" a singular voice among them would propose.

"So say we all!" the rest of their voices would boom in unison, resonating through the great hall whenever their leader unveiled any new mission.

The first of the knights' human rulers Ben had encountered was a slight but vicious man by the name of Enoch. Ben had long since defeated him, and he'd been usurped by a far more intimidating, three-horned, silver-armored knight known as the Forever King. He too was no match for Ben Tennyson and the power of the Omnitrix! Unlike Enoch, however, the Forever King had managed to sneak away undetected, leaving only the empty pieces of his shattered suit of armor behind, and had not been seen nor heard from in quite some time.

The most recent leader of the Forever Knights was a

thin, old man in regal crimson robes, golden crown, and trimmed white goatee. He went by the name of Patrick. But he was nowhere to be found among the assembled knights in the great hall at this moment. Had someone else assumed leadership of the order? And if so, who?

"All hail our once and Forever King!" the knights chanted, thrusting their energy swords high into the air in royal salute.

A dark helmeted figure stepped out from behind the draperies on the altar, basking in the adulation of his followers.

Blah, blah, blah." Kevin made his empty hand talk like a puppet. "Talk to the hand."

He was completely human in appearance now, wearing his ID mask to hide his true features, as he kicked back on the hood of his green muscle car, his legs stretched along the wide black racing stripe, his back against the windshield. Kevin took a slurp from the drinking straw of the white Styrofoam cup in his hand and made a face. "Ugh, blueberry bok choy. This one's yours, Tennyson."

Ben and Kevin were in the parking lot of their favorite local hangout, Mr. Smoothy. Ben reached over and switched cups with Kevin. He swapped out the used straw for a fresh one, announcing, "Don't want any germs."

"You turn into some of the most hideous creatures in the entire galaxy, and you're worried about sharing a straw?" Kevin asked incredulously.

"If it makes you feel any better, I wouldn't share a straw with Swampfire either," shrugged Ben, referring to his stinky, gas-laden, Methanosian form. (Swampfire smelled like rotten eggs.)

"Yeah, that guy's really good in a fight all right, but he does kind of reek, Ben." Kevin opened the lid of his cup this time, peeked inside, and took a whiff to confirm its contents before taking a sip.

"Where's Gwen?" asked Ben between slurps. "I thought she was coming with you?"

"She ditched me," Kevin pouted. "Said she had something important she needed to do. She says that a lot lately."

Ben scratched his chin thoughtfully. "You don't think she—"

"No!" Kevin interrupted, assuming that Ben was going to say that Gwen was obviously getting ready to break up with him.

"No? You don't think she's doing research on that alien artifact we found?" Ben asked quizzically.

"Oh, that. Yeah. Sure. That's got to be what she's doing. What else?" Kevin backpedaled. He slid off the car's hood and opened the passenger side door. This was Kevin's second car of its kind, actually. The first one had been a casualty of the War of the Worlds against the HighBreed. After sacrificing his beloved ride to save Earth—and, let's face it, nothing less would have ever gotten him to do such a thing—Kevin had managed to find this replacement at the local auto show. He'd lovingly restored it to a condition even better than the original. It was all tricked out with cherry rims, sweet vintage chrome accents, and loads and loads of hidden alien tech.

Inside the glove compartment, crammed in a nest of unpaid speeding tickets, sat the alien artifact. Kevin picked it up.

"Careful with that thing." Ben stayed well clear of it.

"It doesn't affect me, remember? No big." Kevin turned it over in his hands. "One of the advantages of being a freak, I guess."

"You mentioned you might have heard of this thing before," Ben reminded him.

"It was a long time ago, back when I was in the Null Void," Kevin explained. "Probably not even the same thing. The artifact I heard about wasn't this small. That might not have even been real, though. Convicts are big talkers."

Ben nodded in understanding. There was a large part of Kevin's life that Ben and Gwen knew absolutely nothing about.

Five years ago, when Kevin was still their mortal enemy, he had been captured and imprisoned in another dimension known as the Null Void, the ultimate punishment for the most hardened and irredeemable criminals. Back then, Kevin certainly fit that description.

What exactly had happened to Kevin while he was in the Null Void all those years—and how he had managed to escape—remained a mystery to this day. Ben still hoped Kevin would tell him and Gwen about it at some point. But Ben never brought up the subject. Sometimes he even managed to forget this was the same "Kevin 11" who had fought him so savagely as a child. Every once in a while, though, Kevin would mention something from during his five years in the Null Void, and Ben's curiosity would be piqued once again.

"What if this is a piece that was broken off the same artifact you heard about in the Null Void?" Ben asked.

"Does it matter?" Kevin countered dismissively.

"Whatever it is, we got it away from those Forever Knights. Problem solved." He stuffed the artifact back into the glove compartment and rapped his fingers on the roof of his car impatiently. "Where the heck is Gwen? How much research can one person possibly stand?"

"You'd be surprised," Gwen said, hovering in the lotus position on a manna energy platform in the air behind Kevin. She took a sip of her smoothy, then demurely wiped her mouth with a napkin. "Come on. You guys aren't going to want to miss this."

The outside of the Bellwood Museum was draped with large hanging banners promoting its latest exhibit: "Mysteries from Outer Space!"

Glancing at the crowd lining up to enter the exhibit, Ben instinctively pulled the left sleeve of his jacket down over the Omnitrix. Nobody knew about his own secret from outer space, and he sure wanted to keep it that way.

"I'm not much for museums, Gwen," Kevin shifted uncomfortably as they pulled up in his car. Then he shook his head. *Great,* he thought. *Now she'll be wanting to date some fancy intellectual guy instead of me.*

"I think you'll be interested in this particular exhibit," Gwen said, pointing to one banner in particular.

According to the posters, chunks of meteorites and other interstellar debris that had made their way to Earth over the years had been collected together for display. It was an attempt to interest the public in celestial study and separating fact from fiction. Scientists and scholars had examined and identified all the objects on display. All but one.

"And I think you can guess what that is," Gwen said.

"Another piece in our puzzle!" Ben answered excitedly.

It was true. Gwen had discovered a second alien artifact much like the one that sat buried in Kevin's glove compartment right now. Maybe they fit together into the single larger object Kevin had heard about in the Null Void years ago.

"Of all the places in the universe it could be, how did you know it would be here in the museum?" Kevin asked.

Gwen held up her Mr. Smoothy napkin. On the back, there was an ad for the museum's exhibit that included a picture of the alien artifact.

"My kind of research," Ben smiled.

Kevin started to get out of the car, but Gwen put a hand on his shoulder.

"We're not going in?" Kevin said a little irritated. "So what do we do now?"

Gwen responded, "We wait."

The sun slowly set in the west, casting a bluish tinge over Kevin's car, which still sat silently parked across the street from the museum. As the last of the museum patrons departed for the night, the parking lot emptied out. The lights inside the museum dimmed.

"Now?" Kevin asked.

"Not yet," Gwen said, staring intensely at the museum. Her eyes glowed with magenta manna energy. This was Gwen's way of sensing something.

Gwen had inherited her amazing energy-manipulating abilities from her and Ben's paternal grandmother, Grandpa Max's wife, Verdona, who happened to be an energy being from a distant planet called Anodyne. Not too long ago, Verdona had returned to Earth and met Ben and Gwen for the very first time. She explained that alien powers sometimes skip a generation: that's why neither Ben nor Gwen's fathers had inherited their mother's otherworldly abilities. But Gwen's father had passed Verdona's genetic code on to his daughter, Gwen. And so it finally came to light that what ten-year-old Gwen used to mistake for magical powers was actually her latent alien nature coming to the surface.

Now one of the ways Gwen was able to use her alien abilities was to tap into the life force, or manna, of any living thing. If she could get a bead on its energy signature, she could track it anywhere in the universe. Or sense its presence nearby.

Sitting in Kevin's car, Gwen's eyes glowed a fierce magenta as she concentrated on the museum.

Ben, bored by all the waiting, idly flipped the lock on the car door up and down, up and down.

Click, clunk. Click, clunk.

Kevin shot him an irritated look.

Click, clunk. Click, clunk.

"Dude!"

"Sorry," Ben realized what he had been doing and stopped. He had a habit of flicking the car door lock to pass the time whenever they were on a stakeout. It drove Kevin absolutely crazy.

Maybe that was why Ben kept doing it.

"They're here," Gwen said ominously. Her glowing eyes blinked and returned to normal.

"Why do we care about this alien artifact again?" Kevin took off his ID mask. He wanted to be battle-ready for any trouble they might run into. "If you guys won't let me sell it, what good is it?"

"Put it back on for now," Gwen advised him gently, gesturing toward his ID mask. "We don't want to draw any unnecessary attention."

"Yeah," Kevin replied, embarrassed that Gwen had come right out and asked him to cover up his hideousness. He replaced his mask. "Wouldn't want anybody to have to look at me."

As the three teens climbed out of the car, there was a flicker behind one of the museum windows. Someone was watching their every move.

CHAPTER FIVE

Inside the museum, all was quiet and still. Bathed in the dim emergency light, all the mannequins and artifacts on display seemed to take on an eerie life of their own. Dinosaur bones, mummy sarcophagi, and terracotta warriors—all were allocated to their own areas of the museum, grouped by subject matter. In one particular wing, a puffy white astronaut posed by his lunar rover under a banner welcoming visitors to the wonderful world of space exploration. This was the place.

From the crack beneath the locked double doors at the front of the museum, a goopy green slime slowly seeped in and spread out over the polished marble floor of the lobby. Ew! The janitor wasn't going to like this mess, whatever it was.

With a flash of green energy, the puddle of goo suddenly transformed into the familiar figure of Ben Tennyson. He unlocked the door from the inside for Kevin and Gwen, who slipped in behind him.

"If you ever want to get out of the hero business," Kevin clapped Ben on the shoulder as he passed, "Goop's got a great career in breaking and entering."

"Not funny, Kevin," Ben said seriously. He would never use his powers that way. Even sneaking into the museum at night like this made him uncomfortable. He reached into his pocket and guiltily left some money in the donations jar. "Why couldn't we just buy a ticket during the day, Gwen?"

"Because the customers or staff might see you use the Omnitrix," she answered.

"If I could've just walked through the front door with a ticket," Ben shrugged his shoulders, "I wouldn't have needed to transform."

"Don't be so sure about that," Kevin called out, indicating dozens of suits of armor lining the corridor directly in front of them. "It's the Forever Knights!"

As Ben reached for the Omnitrix, Kevin yanked off his ID mask, revealing his multi-material physique. He bolted down the corridor, growing both of his metallic hands into giant claws, and raked at the rows of suits of armor on either side of him.

Every suit of armor he struck clattered to the floor, empty. The resounding cacophony echoed loudly throughout the entire museum, room by room. Finally, after what seemed like ages, it died down and all was quiet again.

"There's nobody in them," Gwen said, her eyes glowing with magenta manna energy, sensing no life forms there.

"Yeah, I got that," Kevin replied sheepishly, morphing his hands back to normal, then replacing his ID mask. "You could've said something before."

Ben put away the Omnitrix. "I was sure the Forever Knights would be here to try to steal that artifact."

"Me too," said Gwen, looking around nervously. "But unless something's blocking my ability to sense their manna, there's nobody here but us."

"What if they've already got the artifact?" Ben asked worriedly, hurrying down the hall, following the signs to the correct exhibit room.

On display among real moon rocks, a recreation of a meteor crater, and old-fashioned weather balloons with dioramas debunking common misinformation and conspiracy theories about UFO sightings and alien life forms, sat an artifact similar to the one now stashed unceremoniously in the glove compartment of Kevin's car. Unlike the other objects on display, a big sign beside the unidentified alien artifact read, "Fact or fiction?" This piece was jagged on different sides than the first one the teens had encountered, but was made of the same strange material and had the same kind of incomplete alien glyphs inscribed in it. Clearly the two pieces fit together.

"Kevin? Do the honors?" Ben said with a sweep of his arm toward the display. If this piece had powers anything like its twin, he and Gwen sure weren't going to make the same mistake as last time.

Kevin removed his ID mask and reached for the artifact with the protection of his craggy inhuman hand.

"Ah!" screamed Kevin in pain, falling to his gnarled knees.

Gwen ignited two circles of magenta energy around her hands and, with a grunt of effort, fired a shield between Kevin and the alien artifact.

Unlike the last piece they had encountered, this one

did not cause her energy to dissipate. So apparently this particular piece was affecting Kevin, but not her. Would it still affect Ben?

Ben and Gwen inched toward the injured Kevin. Before they could reach him, several suits of armor stepped out of the darkness from behind the artifact. They were armed with laser lances!

"Forever Knights!" Ben shouted out in surprise.

"Medieval stuff goes in the other room," Kevin muttered sarcastically, struggling to get to his feet. "Not cool confusing the school kids."

"The alien thingamabob must have been blocking my ability to sense their life forces," Gwen deduced, shielding herself, Ben, and Kevin from the knights' laser fire.

"Make with the hero time, Ben!" Kevin prompted.

Ben dialed the Omnitrix and quickly scrolled through a series of semi-transparent green, 3-D holographic images projected up from the watch face: Brain Storm, Humungousaur, Rath. He selected the perfect alien genoarchetype to use in a fight against tin-can-clad guys like these pesky Forever Knights.

"Come on, Lodestar!"

Ben slammed a palm on the Omnitrix and was instantly bathed in the intense green glow of the watch's otherworldly power. He felt his body begin to change on a molecular level as the DNA in the watch's database replaced his own. It was an indescribable sensation. His bones, his muscles, even his brain were altered in ways that only Azmuth truly understood. In a moment, there was no visible sign of Ben Tennyson. In his place now stood a mighty alien form, who, when the transformation was complete, announced his presence by name.

"Echo Echo!" the diminutive white creature stated in a chirpy, electronically enhanced voice.

"Ah, man!" Echo Echo frowned, looking down at himself in disappointment. "We never should have messed with the Omnitrix, Kevin."

"Tell me about it," Kevin mumbled, averting his gaze from Gwen.

"Keep them busy, Ben!" Gwen called out. "I've got to protect the artifact."

"Ahem," said Kevin, clearing his throat.

"And Kevin," Gwen added.

"*Sounds* like a plan to me!" Echo Echo chimed. Like Big Chill, Echo Echo loved making puns about his abilities. The little Sonorosian was tiny but mighty, with the uncanny capacity to amplify sound to a painful degree and use it as a weapon.

"Wooooo!" Echo Echo opened his mouth wide and bellowed with such force that several of the Forever Knights were blown backward and right out the open window they'd come through.

Others were forced to drop their laser lances and make a run for it. "Run away! Run away!" they sang out.

But still others advanced on the small creature. "There's too many of them for me to handle!" Echo Echo cried. Then he chuckled, realizing what he was saying. "Oh. Right."

Just as an echo repeats sound, so Echo Echo could repeat himself by generating absolutely identical duplicates of himself. Taking a running start, he doubled into two, then four, then eight, all without breaking stride!

The Echo Echoes quickly surrounded the remaining Forever Knights. They put their hands on their hips triumphantly.

The Forever Knights burst into hearty laughter. They were hardly trapped. Armored and gigantic, they towered over their tiny captors. One knight prepared to kick an Echo Echo out of the way.

"Wall! Of! Sound!" Echo Echo's eight identical selves bellowed, creating a barrage of powerful invisible audio waves that buffeted the knights in place. Their metallic suits of armor rang in harmony like a chorus of wind chimes.

"Hey," one Echo Echo said with a smile.

"Check us out!" another Echo Echo continued.

"We're musicians!" a third Echo Echo chuckled.

With that, they began taking turns blasting one knight at a time, each suit of armor producing a different note. They were playing a little tune.

"It's the *Sumo Slammers'* theme song," one of the Echo Echoes explained proudly.

That was Ben's favorite TV show of all time. He knew the song by heart. He had practically memorized the lyrics in Japanese too, even though he had no idea what he was saying.

"Quit fooling around, Ben, and take them out!" groaned Kevin, still stunned from his surprise zap of energy from the alien artifact.

"Right!" an Echo Echo chirped.

"Okay!" another one chimed in.

"Sorry!" yet another one offered.

"Got carried away!" a fourth one finished.

The eight Echo Echoes merged down into one. The one remaining little alien slapped the Omnitrix symbol on his chest, transforming in a flash of green light from Ben's smallest available alien form into his largest.

"Waybig!" the enormous creature called out. And he sure was! Even in a crouch, Waybig's head scraped the cathedral ceiling of the museum chamber.

"Dude!" weakened Kevin said with admiration. "Good call!"

"I was going for Cannonbolt," Waybig admitted with a shrug. "But this'll do just fine."

The remaining Forever Knights tilted their helmeted heads to look up at Waybig. Waybig waved demurely down at them, wiggling just the tips of his gigantic fingers.

One knight drew his blue-bladed energy sword. But another, more sensible, knight patted his friend's gauntlet to make him put the sword away.

"Yeah, I think you guys probably want to run away now," Waybig declared, grinning. He reached down with one of his gigantic hands, wide enough to scoop them all up in one grasp.

The knights looked at each other and, without even bothering with their signature call of retreat, ran away.

"Verily the Forever King shall be most displeased," one knight said grimly to the other.

"Both of the missing pieces he seeks hath fallen into yon enemies' hands," the second one agreed.

"On the contrary," a third knight replied. "Everything doth proceed exactly according to the Forever King's plan."

CHAPTER SIX

Gwen held the second alien artifact shard they'd found in front of her. She let go of it, and it stayed hovering there in the same spot in the air. Gwen's eyes glowed with magenta manna power as she continued to stare at the object, causing it to slowly rotate in space. She put her fingertips to her temples and concentrated.

"Anything yet?" Kevin asked, sliding out from under his car. They were in Kevin's garage, where he was taking the opportunity to install some more alien tech in his ride. His normal human face meant that he was wearing his ID mask again.

The alien artifact clattered to the unfinished cement floor of the garage.

"Not if you keep interrupting me," Gwen sighed in exasperation. She was trying to get a manna signature reading off the item.

Ben paced back and forth tensely. "What are you trying to sense exactly?"

"The owner of the last piece," Gwen replied, eyes squinted shut. "But all I keep seeing is," she paused, "me."

"You're the last person who touched that piece," Ben pointed out helpfully. "So you're probably sensing your own manna."

Gwen opened her eyes. He was right.

"Have you tried the other one?" Ben offered.

"I can't touch it," Gwen reminded him.

"But I can." Kevin climbed into his car, and after the sound of crinkling papers, emerged with the first alien artifact they had found.

"Keep both those things away from me," Ben took a step back and covered the Omnitrix protectively. "I can't touch either of them." He'd tried earlier, and had the same reaction to this piece as he'd had to the first. "Wonder if it has something to do with the Omnitrix."

"I'd say that's a good bet," Kevin replied.

Kevin held his artifact up in front of Gwen, though

40

not too close. She concentrated on it and, in doing so, made her piece drift up from the floor and hover again. It was bathed in a steady magenta glow.

Suddenly, Kevin's piece sprang from his hand and floated beside the other, encapsulated in its light. He gasped in surprise.

"You okay, Gwen? It's not hurting you, is it?" Kevin asked worriedly.

"No," Gwen answered, eyes aglow. "I'm not making contact with it directly. Somehow my energy's flowing through my piece into yours."

"Whoa," Ben exhaled, gazing in awe upon the glowing artifacts floating in the air.

The two items did not interlock, but seeing them side by side like this, it was easy to see now how they would fit together and where a third missing piece should go. The glyphs engraved on the two pieces flashed eerily, and Kevin could make out some of the complete alien words now.

"'When darkness rises,'" he read slowly, "'night falls.'"

"Sounds like an alien fortune cookie," chuckled Ben, trying to lighten the intense mood.

"Kind of a lame fortune," Kevin agreed.

"Maybe you're reading it wrong," Ben suggested.

Gwen suddenly got a flash of a vision that no one else in the room saw: She saw the missing piece in pink manna energy form filling the blank with the others in the air in front of her!

"The missing piece!" she cried.

"Where?" Ben looked around startled.

For a split second, Gwen caught a glimpse of the location of the missing piece, and then it was gone.

The glow died out around the hovering artifacts, and they both fell to the garage floor. With a moan, Gwen collapsed from exertion.

"Gwen!" Kevin dove toward her and gathered her up in his arms.

Gwen smiled weakly at him. "I know where the missing piece is," she said.

A sonic boom ripped through the atmosphere as Ben's fastest alien form, Jet Ray, dove down from the gathering gray storm clouds above a lonely hillside. Jet Ray was an Aerophibian, equally at home in the air and in the water, much like an amphibian on Earth lives both on land and in the water. Whenever Ben needed to get anywhere fast, he turned into Jet Ray. He carried Gwen and Kevin, who hung on for dear life.

"Nice of the Omnitrix to turn you into the alien you actually wanted, huh," Kevin shouted over the sound of the rushing wind.

"Good thing I didn't become Upchuck, or we'd still be walking," Jet Ray quipped.

"You should try changing into some alien you *don't* want and see if you can trick the Omnitrix into making you into the one you *do*," Kevin pondered.

"It doesn't really work like that," Jet Ray responded in his screechy voice. "I don't think the Omnitrix can think."

"You think?" Kevin kidded.

Gwen, eyes aglow, was ignoring their in-flight banter. She was too busy scanning the landscape for any sign of—

"There!" Gwen shouted, interrupting her own thoughts. She pointed to a large dark area on the ground below.

As Jet Ray's feet touched the ground, he transformed into Ben. He crumpled under the weight of his two friends, and they all landed together in a heap.

"Oof! Sorry for the rough landing. Thank you for flying Jet Ray airlines," Ben joked.

"Oh, dude. Seriously?" Kevin said as he stood up, dusting himself off.

"I said sorry," Ben repeated.

"Not you. That." Kevin was staring past Ben at the large stone fortress at which they'd arrived.

"It's what I saw in my vision of the missing part of the alien artifact," Gwen explained. "The thief's own manna on it must have led me here."

Gwen had the one piece she could touch in her school bag on her back now. Kevin had his stashed in a satchel over his shoulder.

"The Forever Knights' fortress. Surprise, surprise," Ben nodded.

"Anybody else thinking 'trap'?" Kevin frowned.

Ben, Gwen, and Kevin crept along the ramparts on top of the castle, looking for the best way to sneak in.

"Why don't we just use the front door?" Ben wondered. "I'll turn into Humungousaur, the Forever Knights will run away, we'll retrieve the piece of the artifact they stole, and we're back at Mr. Smoothy's celebrating before you know it."

"Element of surprise," Kevin whispered. "Sh."

Suddenly the solid stone gave way beneath their feet. They'd stumbled onto a secret passageway!

"Whoa!" the three teenagers cried in surprise, noisily tumbling down into the fortress below.

"So much for the element of surprise," Ben said.

"Hey, I got us in, didn't I?" Kevin shrugged. He was the kind of guy who got results. How he arrived at those results didn't matter much to him.

"This way," Gwen whispered, igniting a tiny ball of magenta energy in front of them.

As they snuck past one of the magnificent paintings on the wall of a long-ago king, its blue eyes watched them go.

"Where are all the knights?" wondered Ben. He'd never seen their headquarters so empty.

"Probably out boosting more alien tech," Kevin shrugged.

"Careful, though," Gwen warned. "The thief's got to be here somewhere, or I wouldn't have been able to track his manna to the castle."

Following Gwen's energy senses, they made their way silently through the spookily vacant fortress down into the musty dungeons. When it came to recreating a medieval setting, the Forever Knights definitely went all out.

"You sure that thing knows where it's going?" Kevin asked. "There's nobody way down here."

"Help me!" cried out a muffled voice from somewhere deep inside the dungeon.

They all heard it.

"Now the Forever Knights are taking prisoners?" Ben frowned. "I thought they were just thieves."

"Well, they did hold that dragon prisoner for a thousand years," Kevin pointed out matter-of-factly. He morphed his hand into a giant stone mallet and prepared to strike the door.

"Good point," Ben admitted, then leaped into action himself. "I got this. It's hero time!"

He dialed the Omnitrix and slammed the watch face, silently hoping for Humungousaur. A burst of green energy engulfed him. He felt his body go completely limp as his bones and muscles turns to mush, the DNA of a member of the shape-shifting Polymorph species replacing his own. A little flying saucer buzzed in and used its gravity-generating field to pull the green puddle that was Ben into an upright humanoid shape.

"Goop!" he announced in a high-pitched squeal. "Aw, no Humungousaur? He could've bashed any dungeon door off its hinges with his pinky finger."

"Yeah, but Goop's got experience in B&E, remember?" Kevin reminded Ben.

"B&E?" Goop squeaked.

"Breaking and entering," Kevin translated.

Goop splashed down into a puddle once again, slid under the cell door, and congealed back into his upright shape on the other side. Once there, he froze, amazed at what he'd found.

"What's going on in there?" Gwen called, igniting energy spheres around her hands to strike the door down herself.

Inside the cell, Goop just stared silently in shock.

On his knees, chained to the wall in energy restraints was a black-clad prisoner, his face hidden behind a familiar black iron mask.

It was their old enemy, Darkstar!

CHAPTER SEVEN

Michael?" Ben asked, appearing in a flash of green light where Goop had previously stood. "What are you doing here?"

"Ben Tennyson," Darkstar intoned in that unsettlingly calm way of his. "Forgive me if I don't get up."

Michael Morningstar had been a handsome, charismatic blond with amazing energy-based powers. All the teenage girls at his prep school had adored him. Ben, Gwen, and Kevin had first made his acquaintance when these same schoolgirls began turning up haggard and wan, with strange, round, jagged markings on their arms. They were all obsessed with finding Michael.

Ben and his friends had discovered that Michael's father was a Plumber, and Michael himself had amassed an impressive collection of surveillance technology to keep an eye out for alien trouble in the area. Because of this, Ben had been very excited to recruit him onto their burgeoning Alien Force team, but Kevin hadn't been so sure. He didn't like the way Gwen had been acting since Michael first showed up. Kevin and Gwen hadn't been officially dating back then, but that didn't stop Kevin from being jealous of the attention Gwen was paying this newcomer.

It turned out Kevin's suspicions weren't entirely unfounded. Michael had set his sights on Gwen—"lovely Gwen," as he always referred to her—because he had been able to sense her powerful Anodite nature. In order to retain his youthful appearance, Michael Morningstar needed to feed off the life force of others. He was an energy vampire. It had taken all the strength Gwen had to fight back against him, and it was his own legion of energy-sapped schoolgirl zombies that were his ultimate undoing. They turned on him, draining Michael of all the life force he had stolen from them and then some, leaving him a shriveled gray carcass of his former handsome self.

From then on, Michael Morningstar, grotesque and withered, went by the name Darkstar. No longer beautiful, Michael hid his face from the world under a black iron mask, with only slits at the eyes and mouth. As Darkstar, he had tried to exact revenge against Ben and his friends for the monstrous state in which they'd left him, but he had been defeated once again. This time, he was sentenced to the Null Void prison dimension by a Plumber named Magister Prior Gilhil.

However, during the desperate era of the War of the Worlds, Ben and his Alien Force team needed help against the HighBreed's massive invading forces, so Ben and his friends had released Darkstar from the Null Void on the condition that he help them in their battle against the HighBreed. Once in their dimension, Darkstar would have been just as doomed by the HighBreed as every other living being in the galaxy. He had no choice but to fight by the side of his former enemies. But as soon as the battle was over, he'd slipped away.

Now, in the dungeon beneath the Forever Knight's castle, the door of Darkstar's cell glowed with magenta energy. After a beat, Kevin's stone hammer fist came crashing through the portal's compromised structure.

"After you," Kevin offered gallantly, as he followed Gwen into the cell.

"Ah, the lovely Gwen," Darkstar breathed.

"Michael?" Gwen stared at him incredulously. "You're a prisoner of the Forever Knights? But how? They couldn't possibly overpower you."

"You flatter me," Darkstar bowed. "But I am afraid the Forever Knights are no longer to be underestimated," he paused for dramatic effect, "under the leadership of their Forever King."

"That guy's back?" Ben asked, recognizing the name of his old enemy. "He hasn't been around since I was a kid."

"Perhaps the Forever King has been in hiding, biding his time, growing stronger," Darkstar pondered. "Revenge is a powerful motivator."

"You would know," Kevin said, frowning.

"Levin," Darkstar uttered smoothly, observing Kevin's appearance. "You're looking well. Not."

Kevin self-consciously put his ID mask back on.

Gwen put a supportive hand on Kevin's shoulder. He shrugged it off. This did not go unnoticed by Darkstar.

"What does the Forever King have against you?" asked Ben.

"Not 'against' me. *For* me. To do," Darkstar explained. "The Forever King apparently has a piece of a powerful alien artifact in his possession that no one is able to touch but me."

Ben, Gwen, and Kevin exchanged looks. They all had the same thought: Darkstar's powers must somehow protect him from the final section of the artifact, the way Kevin's protected him from a piece, and Gwen's from another. Ben couldn't help but feel a little left out.

Gwen instinctively put her hand on the shoulder strap of her book bag that contained her piece, and Kevin's thumbs fumbled with the flap on the satchel at his side holding his.

"If you release me, I'll show you where it is," Darkstar stated.

"Since you're the only one who can touch it, if you promise to help get its power out of the hands of the Forever Knights, we'll release you," Ben countered.

"Tennyson, I'm not sure that's a good—"

"Done," Darkstar agreed.

"—idea," Kevin finished with a sigh.

CHAPTER EIGHT

This way," Darkstar said, as he strode confidently down the corridors of the castle. His black boots clicked on the stone floors, and the light from wall-mounted candelabrum flickered on the buckles of the three belts banded around his abdomen. Behind the slits in his iron mask, his eyes never blinked.

"Where are all the knights?" Ben looked around warily as he followed.

"In the years without a strong leader, their numbers have dwindled," Darkstar explained. "But with the return of the Forever King, their ranks will surely expand."

Gwen and Kevin lagged behind, whispering among themselves.

"I don't trust this guy," Kevin said flatly.

"You don't trust anybody," Gwen whispered back. "But in this case, I agree with you. Keep your eyes open."

Darkstar led them to the great hall. The stained glass windows lining the chamber depicted scenes of glorious days of chivalry gone by. Grand tapestries were woven with dramatic images of brave knights slaying dragons. On the altar, an ornate throne was draped in regal crimson vestments: the seat of power of the returned Forever King.

"It's here, behind the throne," Darkstar said, quickening his stride. "The Forever King prefers to keep it close to him at all times."

"Not *all* times," Kevin remarked. "Dude's not even here."

Ben, Gwen, and Kevin followed Darkstar down the center aisle of the great hall and up onto the altar. From behind the throne, Darkstar produced a jeweled chest.

"That's got to be worth a couple of bucks," Kevin nodded, impressed.

"A mere trinket," Darkstar retorted. "The true treasure is what lies inside."

Darkstar held the ornate cube in front of his chest

and opened its doors with a flourish. A sudden blinding flash of energy poured out of the small box and filled the expansive castle chamber. Inside the case Darkstar was holding, nearly obscured by the power it was emitting, Ben could make out the contours of the third and final piece of the mysterious alien artifact.

"You've got it!" Ben cried excitedly. "Great." He started down the aisle toward the exit and called back to the others. "Come on, let's get it out of here."

"I think not," Darkstar said coldly.

The alien artifact hidden in Gwen's backpack suddenly sprang to life, glowing right through her bag. The piece in Kevin's satchel did the same.

"I believe you two have something for me," Darkstar taunted.

The force emanating from Gwen's artifact continued to grow until it completely surrounded her. She tried to fire up a manna energy attack, but her powers were being suppressed by the artifact.

"Can't . . . move . . ." Gwen grunted.

Kevin too was now trapped within the energy expanding from his artifact, rendering his powers useless as well. He struggled, growling angrily at Darkstar, "Not cool, dude!"

Out in the aisle, Ben had already called up a creature on the dial of the Omnitrix and was poised to slap it to activate the transformation.

"Uh uh uh," Darkstar wagged a gloved finger at Ben, then gestured toward his two hostages.

Ben froze, but kept the Omnitrix at the ready.

Darkstar leaped up and stood on the arms of the throne.

"I knew all along you had the other two pieces with you," Darkstar said smugly. "In fact, I've just been waiting for you to bring them to me."

Suddenly, out from under the gothic archway of every darkened alcove lining the length of the chamber stepped a seemingly endless number of Forever Knights! One after the other, they filed in, filling the great hall.

"All hail our once and Forever King!" the knights chanted, raising their blue-bladed energy swords in the air.

"You?" cried Ben from across the chamber. He was surrounded by a sea of Forever Knights as Darkstar loomed over the paralyzed Gwen and Kevin. "*You're* the new Forever King?"

CHAPTER NINE

I am!" announced Darkstar triumphantly. "And my growing loyal legions of Forever Knights hear and obey the every command of their Forever King without question!"

"All hail our once and Forever King!" On cue, the knights' voices rang out again. They raised their laser swords in salute.

"I thought you said the Forever Knights' ranks were dwindling?" shouted Ben.

"I lied," Darkstar stated flatly.

The evidence was all around Ben. With a new, charismatic leader like Darkstar on board, recruitment in the Forever Knights was at an all-time high!

Ben found himself surrounded by scores of rank and file knights a head taller than he, jostling in his eye-line, but never for one instant did he take his eye off Darkstar.

Up on the altar, his feet on the arms of throne, Darkstar held aloft the glowing box containing his piece of the powerful alien artifact.

"Yes, all hail me!" Darkstar said heartily.

"Take him out, Ben! Now!" Kevin moaned.

Gwen and Kevin floated in the air on either side of Darkstar's throne, helplessly trapped in separate spheres of crackling energy generated by their respective pieces of the alien artifact.

"You've got to stop him, Ben," Gwen murmured. "Don't worry about us."

Ben kept his right hand hovering over the Omnitrix, twitching at the ready. He didn't want to give Darkstar a reason to destroy his friends, but as soon as Darkstar gave him an opening, it was going to be hero time all over this place!

"At my bidding, my loyal knights scoured the world to locate the alien artifact I require," Darkstar said, nodding approvingly at his legions. "But it had been broken and the pieces scattered, in an unsuccessful attempt to deter its use, I suppose," he mused. "The unstable energy residing in each of the pieces made them impossible to be handled by just anybody. But I was able to get around that. . . ."

Darkstar grinned up at the weakened forms of Kevin and Gwen hovering within their masses of energy. "Thanks to my unwitting assistants here," he finished cruelly.

Ben could not fathom, even as mission-oriented as the Forever Knights always were, that they could possibly want to be a part of this.

"What's the matter with you knights?" Ben shouted at the sea of suits of armor around him, though the focus of his steely gaze never wavered from Darkstar. "Why are you helping this guy?"

The knights seemed to not even hear Ben. They just continued staring fixedly at the altar. Their gaze never faltered from Darkstar.

"All hail our once and Forever King!" they chanted yet again.

"Yeah, you said that already," said Ben, suspiciously. "What are you, robots or something?"

"Or something," cackled Darkstar.

All over the chamber, dozens of Forever Knights

lifted the visors on their helmets, revealing horrifying, shriveled, nightmarish visages inside! Ben's eyes widened in disbelief. Inside their imprisoning cocoons of energy, Kevin and Gwen looked on in terror.

"Behold my army of energy zombies!" Darkstar bellowed.

Ben could barely believe what he was seeing. Instead of normal human beings inside the suits of armor, every single one of these Forever Knights had the same sickly pallor, sunken eyes, and wrinkled gray skin as Darkstar!

"You've absorbed all of their life forces!" Ben cried out in dismay.

"Indeed!" Darkstar cried back victoriously.

He threw off his own black iron mask, revealing the handsome young face of Michael Morningstar!

"Gaze upon this, the face of victory!" Michael sang out, his blue eyes twinkling against his impeccable skin and movie-star blond hair.

"So you've already got your youth back," Ben said, trying to reason with him. "What do you need to assemble the artifact for?"

"The alien energy conduit will amplify my power," Michael explained exultantly, "allowing me to absorb all of the life force energy in the world." He paused for dramatic effect. "Thanks to these artifacts, I can live forever!"

With that, Darkstar heaved the box containing his piece of the artifact into the air between Gwen and Kevin. Once they were in such close proximity, the three severed pieces of the alien artifact generated a spectacular circuit of piercing electricity that arced through the air between them, pulling the three long separated pieces together!

The moment the box left Michael's hands, Ben seized the opportunity to act. He would get only one shot at this. He'd better make it count! He slammed his hand on the Omnitrix and disappeared in a flash of green light.

Deep inside Ben's cells, his basic genetic structure went through a startling metamorphosis. Crystalline alien material replicated within him, increasing his mass, squaring his features, and hardening his surface area. When the green glow faded, the creature now standing there called out his name.

"Diamondhead!" he announced.

As soon as he realized which creature he'd become, he pumped his fist in the air. "Yeah, baby!"

Diamondhead was one of Ben's original alien forms,

from back when he was a kid. A Petrosapien ("petro" meaning rock and "sapien" meaning an intelligent life form), this creature's physical structure was harder than a diamond, rendering him invulnerable to most damage. But the Omnitrix had reset when Ben first put it on again at age fifteen, and Diamondhead had no longer been among his available transformations. However, because of a recent tragic accident with Ben's similar geno-arche-type—a Chrystalsapien named ChromaStone—Ben once again had access to its predecessor, Diamondhead. ChromaStone had paid a dire price for that privilege.

Ben didn't have time to dwell on that now, though.

"Hee-yah!" Diamondhead barreled through the throngs of zombified Forever Knights and hurled himself at the cloud of energy massing above the altar!

"Stop him!" Michael commanded, his boyish good looks twisting into uncontrollable rage.

The Forever Knights took up arms in defense of their king! Holding shields emblazoned with the crest of their Order—a sword over the infinity symbol—along with much higher-tech weaponry like laser lances and energy swords, the assembled masses of zombified knights set their sights collectively on a single enemy of the crown: Ben Tennyson.

"Stop him!" the Forever Knights parroted mindlessly, closing in on Diamondhead.

"Don't make me have to hurt you," Diamondhead cautioned, pushing his attackers away as they staggered toward him at a snail's pace.

But these knights were not able to think for themselves. Just as the affected girls from Michael Morningstar's prep school had stalked him with such slavish devotion, so too these Forever Knights he had fed upon would never choose to leave his side. They leveled their laser lances at Diamondhead and fired at point blank range!

"Ah!" Diamondhead cried out. Then Ben remembered the scope of this alien form's powers. "Oh. Right. It's been so long, I almost forgot!"

Since he was made of crystal, Diamondhead was able to absorb all the rays blasted at him. And that is exactly what Ben did now. Then he redirected the energy at the buttresses holding up the cathedral-like ceiling, causing chunks of masonry to rain down on the heavily armored knights.

"Oof!" and "Ugh!" they uttered, their medieval battle gear protecting them from any severe injury.

On the altar, Michael rose into the air, bathed in a golden hue. He was beginning to feel the effects of the assembled artifact, and his powers were increasing.

"Yes!" he cried. "Yes! The power of the world is mine!"

Michael threw his head back and let the massive amounts of life force energy wash over him.

Inside their floating, confining shells of energy, Kevin and Gwen were beginning to change!

"Kevin! Your face!" Gwen called feebly over to Kevin.

"Gwen! Your . . . everything!" Kevin was too busy reacting in horror to what was happening to Gwen to worry about himself. Her face was turning an ashen gray, her flesh was noticeably shriveling, and the red had begun to fade from her hair. Michael Morningstar was stealing her powers!

"Lovely Gwen," Michael grinned wide. The energy vampire had been coveting Gwen's vast stores of Anodite-enhanced manna life force ever since the day they'd met. "So nice of you to finally share."

Kevin's face was also changing, but in a decidedly different way than Gwen's. His craggy hands were smoothing out, and his mixed-material body was becoming singularly human!

"Levin," Michael seethed, "how dare you steal energy

from the artifact to try to make yourself more handsome, like me!"

"Yeah, like I'd want to look anything like you." No matter how weak he was, Kevin could always find enough energy to make a sarcastic remark.

Gwen was fading fast. "Can't . . . hold on . . . much . . . longer. . . ."

Kevin's body was involuntarily absorbing life force energy through the alien conduit, causing his appearance to return to normal and Gwen's decline to accelerate. In other words, Kevin was siphoning energy from Gwen!

"Ah, the poetic justice," Michael said to Gwen. "Levin will be cured just in time to watch you die."

Then he turned to Kevin and added for good measure, "Probably just as well. She clearly couldn't stand to look at you as a monster."

"Why . . . you!" Kevin furiously punched at the energy mass around him, but his soft human hands had no chance against it.

"Hm," Michael grinned, pleased at the pain he'd inflicted without even raising a fist. "Must've struck a nerve."

CHAPTER TEN

"Out of my way, you tin cans!" shouted Diamondhead from the foot of the altar.

Making use of his sharp edges that could cut through almost anything, Diamondhead sliced at the armor of the attacking Forever Knights. Pieces of their suits of armor—a midsection here, a gauntlet there—clattered to the floor, exposing their withered, gray torsos and limbs in places. Now the slow-moving Forever Knights looked even more like zombies than before!

"All hail our once and Forever King!" the knights chanted in monotone.

Floating above the altar, bathed in the invigorating golden glow of the life force energy he'd collected,

Michael Morningstar gave a gentle, farewell salute.

"Goodbye, lovely Gwen," he said, shaking his head wistfully.

Gwen didn't answer. Her gray form hung motionless within the energy field encapsulating her.

"Gwen!" Kevin cried out in anguish, clawing futilely at his own energy prison.

Suddenly, a huge, hulking figure burst through the mass of electricity arcing between Kevin, Gwen, and Michael!

"Ahhhh!" Diamondhead bellowed. All the energy was now flowing into him instead!

At the very moment Diamondhead interrupted the circuit, the force fields holding Kevin and Gwen immediately vanished. They fell to the floor on either side of the throne.

"No!" Michael hollered. His golden aura began to fade a bit. But he didn't want to break his connection with the assembled alien artifact still hovering in front of him. "Forever Knights! Seize them!"

The slow-moving Forever Knights trudged toward the altar, firing laser blasts at Diamondhead.

"Can't . . . absorb . . . it . . . all . . . ," Diamondhead strained.

"Give it here!" Kevin called out, kneeling beside the grotesquely deformed Gwen. She was barely breathing now.

"No," Diamondhead grunted with great effort, "I'm absorbing all kinds of energy in tremendous amounts. If she gets hit with all this at once, it'll kill her!"

Kevin looked around frantically. His eyes locked onto the assembled alien artifact that was still shimmering with power in the air above the altar.

Kevin couldn't turn his hands into giant mallets or anvils to break the artifact. He couldn't transform into anything heroic. He had no super powers left. He was just a regular person. All he had was himself. But he knew what he had to do.

"Yaaaaa!" he screamed, leaping up onto the seat of the throne. He scrambled up the throne's high back, then launched himself into the air. He threw his arms around the alien artifact in a midair bear-hug and wrestled it to the floor!

"No!" Michael Morningstar's airborne electrical bond with the artifact had been broken.

"Ahhh!" Kevin screamed in pain. His super-powered self had only been able withstand one part of the artifact without injury. His human self was completely unable to endure any of it. The artifact shot out energy wildly, searing through and illuminating Kevin.

Diamondhead absorbed more laser blasts as they hit him, then swung his arm and sliced right through the alien tech lances of the Forever Knights.

"You guys never learn, do you?" he said, frowning.

"Give all that power to me, Ben!" Michael Morningstar screeched, his blue eyes blazing. "You don't need it. But I do!"

"I wouldn't try that if I were you," Diamondhead warned him, but Michael was undeterred. He aimed golden energy absorption beams at Diamondhead.

Michael strained to draw energy out of the crystalline alien creature, but a Petrosapien like Diamondhead was born for this game.

"What? What's happening?" Michael stammered as Diamondhead's infinitely stronger powers of energy absorption drew the life force out of him!

"Let go of me, Michael!" Diamondhead pleaded with his enemy. "It doesn't have to end like this!"

But it was too late.

"Noooo!" Michael Morningstar wailed in pain and

humiliation as his handsome, youthful features withered away into the sickly, peaked, pale, drawn visage of his alter ego, Darkstar!

"All hail the once and Forever King," the chorus of zombie Forever Knights chanted.

"Aw, shut up!" Darkstar seethed.

Helmetless, his sunken, dark-circled eyes darting beneath the sprigs of wiry gray hair on his head, Darkstar turned and leaped at his last chance to recover his youth.

"Levin! Give me the artifact! Now!" he shrieked, diving wildly through the air at Kevin. Powerful black energy beams shot from his hands.

"Um, no?" Kevin said flatly, surprising Darkstar with a boulder-fist punch right in his unprotected face!

Darkstar landed in a heap behind Kevin. In an instant, he was up again, and racing toward a small door behind the altar.

Kevin spun back around to pick up the alien artifact that had healed him. He had to get it over to Gwen before it was too late for her. But it was gone!

"Michael! Give it back! You can't do this!" Kevin shouted.

"Looking for this?"

Kevin's head snapped around at the sound of Gwen's voice. His eyes widened with shock.

She stood over him, looking just like new, perfectly healed, with the flickering alien artifact floating in the air between her manna energy-protected hands. It was almost out of juice. The alien glyphs were the only parts left glowing on it now.

Kevin was never so happy to see someone alive in his life. He wanted to give Gwen a big hug and tell her how happy he was that she was okay. But being Kevin, he played it cool.

"Just what I was looking for," he said, ignoring the artifact and smiling at Gwen.

Gwen smiled back at him.

At the front of the altar, Diamondhead found himself surrounded by increasingly confused and aggressively despondent Forever Knights.

"Where is he?" one knight asked.

"What have you done with our Forever King?" another demanded.

"Tell us where he is!" yet another pleaded in melo-dramatic desperation.

"Just the like the girls at Michael's prep school," Diamondhead observed.

As the aggressively possessive knights closed in around them, Gwen, Kevin, and Diamondhead formed a circle on the altar. The three-part alien artifact floated in a pink manna field above them. Kevin reached out with his craggy inhuman hand and took hold of his piece of the puzzle. Gwen's glowing eyes fixed on the piece that was hers.

Diamondhead hesitated. "I couldn't touch it before."

"But those were our pieces. And you were Ben," Gwen reminded Diamondhead.

"You cleaned Michael's clock, didn't you?" Kevin put in. "You can take over his section, no prob."

Diamondhead grabbed hold of the piece of the artifact that Darkstar had provided.

Surrounded by desperately clingy, zombified Forever Knights, pining for their absent leader, the three heroes held onto the artifact as its glyphs continued to glow.

"What does it say anyway?" Diamondhead asked Kevin.

Kevin squinted at the alien writing and read the completed translation: "Oh. 'When *Knight* rises, *Darkstar* falls.'"

"You sure about that?" Diamondhead teased.

"No," Kevin said, smiling.

Their powers now intact again, the three friends ripped the alien artifact back into three separate pieces, releasing a circular shock wave of energy that shot out over all the Forever Knights around them.

Bathed in the glow of life force returning to them, the Forever Knights' sickly pallor changed. Their cheeks flushed. Their gnarled fingers grew plump. Their sunken eyes twinkled with life. They stood still a moment, confused.

At last, one of them spoke, pointing at Diamondhead. "Forsooth! An alien creature hath invaded the castle!" he cried.

"Verily we must slay it!" another suggested.

"So say we?" a single voice proposed.

"So say we all!" his comrades thundered in agreement.

The revitalized Forever Knights started to take up arms again against Diamondhead!

"Hold it!" Diamondhead held up his hand, palm forward, in the universal gesture for *'Are you people crazy?'*

Diamondhead touched the Omitrix symbol on his chest. In a flash of green light, he was Ben again. The crowd of Forever Knights let out a collective gasp.

"It's me," Ben reminded them, pointing at the number 10 on his green jacket. "Ben Tennyson."

"That's even worse!" a Forever Knight howled.

Others joined in. "Get out of our castle!"

"Trespassers!"

"Guess you're probably not in line to take over as Forever King anytime soon, huh, Tennyson?" Kevin needled Ben as they hurried out of the castle.

"I wonder who their new leader will be?" pondered Ben.

"I've got some free time," Kevin smirked, taking a step back toward the castle.

Gwen grabbed his elbow. "Uh-uh. Oh no. You're sticking with me, Levin."

Kevin looked at her in surprise, then grinned.

Ben smiled. It was nice to have things back to normal again.

Check out this exclusive
preview from the next
Ben 10 Alien Force chapter
book, *Galaxy Wars.*

No fair! You moved your Pupa an extra space!"

Cumo frowned across the table at his game partner, Cirro. The two tech specialists were on duty at the Intergalactic Communications Center in the orbit of Ventulus, a planet on the outer rim of the Morpho galaxy. Things were slow, and they were goofing off.

Nothing much ever happened at the comm station anyway. Although Ventulus was a technologically advanced planet, the Hedillans who populated it were happy with the way things were, and they didn't do much space traveling. When alien ships came into Ventulus space, they were told very politely to turn around and go home. If that didn't work, the Hedillans used their arsenal of laser cannons to get the point across.

Word got around the galaxy that the Hedillans didn't want any visitors, so the comm station was almost always quiet. Cumo and Cirro were there to fix things that malfunctioned and field any messages that came in.

Most of the time, they played their favorite board game, Existence. The object of the game was to get to the end with the most money and awards for good citizenship. Cirro always won, and Cumo was getting pretty tired of it. He was sure Cirro must be cheating.

"You're seeing things," Cirro told him.

"My eyes are fine," Cumo snapped. His antennae twitched in annoyance. "You're cheating! I know it!"

Cirro flapped his pale white wings, a sign he was getting angry. "I am not! Now take your turn!"

Beep! Beep! Beep! Beep!

"Did you say something?" Cirro asked.

"That wasn't me," Cumo replied. His eyes rotated so he could see behind him. "Well, look at that! It's the radar! We've got company."

Both workers wheeled their metal chairs over to their station. The radar screen showed a large blip moving toward Ventulus. Cirro pressed a button on the control panel in front of him.

"You are entering Ventulus space," he announced. "Please turn around immediately. There are no visitors allowed here."

There was no reply. Cumo went to another screen and started twisting dials.

"I've got a visual," he said. "It's a Pratarian ship!"

"Those ground dwellers?" Cirro asked. "I wonder what brought them out of their holes?"

"They must not have heard you," Cumo said. "Try again."

"Repeat, you are about to enter Ventulus space," Cirro said. "Do not proceed."

But the ship kept coming.

"What do we do now?" Cumo asked.

Cirro flipped through the comm station manual. "It says here to activate the laser cannons."

"Laser cannons?" Cumo asked. "That seems a bit harsh, doesn't it? I mean, maybe they just can't hear us, or—"

BOOM! An explosion rocked the comm station, throwing Cumo and Cirro off of their chairs. They groaned and looked at each other, stunned.

"We're under attack!" Cirro yelled. "Raise the shields!"

Cumo jumped up and frantically pressed buttons on his station. "The shields are down," he reported, his voice rising in panic. "They've been disabled!"

BOOM! Another explosion hit the station. Cumo went flying back against the wall. Cirro ran to him and grabbed his arm.

"We've got to get out of here," he said.

"Right!" Cumo agreed. "The escape pods."

They raced through the comm station, through smoke and sparks, to get to the transport bay. They each jumped in an escape pod as another blast of fire assaulted the station.

Within seconds, they were whipping away from the comm station and racing toward the planet's surface. Cirro made contact with the Hedillan command center.

"General, we are under attack!" he cried. "It's a Pratarian ship."

Cumo's eyes rotated just in time to see the comm station blow up.

"The comm station has been destroyed," Cumo reported.

On the planet's surface, the Hedillan general began

activating the laser cannons. Behind him, Monarch, the Hedillan ruler, seethed with fury.

"The Pratarians will rue the day they attacked Ventulus," he said. "This is war!"

Woo hoo! It's party time!" Ben Tennyson said, climbing out of his car. His sometime girlfriend Julie Yamamoto got out of the passenger seat next to him.

A tall boy with shaggy dark hair emerged from the backseat. "Can somebody remind me again what we're doing here?" Kevin Levin asked.

Gwen Tennyson got out of the car last. "Come on, Kevin, it won't be so bad," said the red-haired teen. She had the same green eyes as her cousin, Ben. "Cooper did help us save Earth once. The least we can do is go to his sixteenth birthday party."

"I didn't know nerds knew how to party," Kevin mumbled.

Ben shrugged. "Hey, I'm not thrilled about this either, but how bad can it be?"

"I spent two days in jail on Athos chained to a methane monster," Kevin replied. "I'm guessing that was more fun than this is going to be."

Ben ran up to the front door and rang the bell. The door was opened by a chubby boy with blond hair and a pimply face. He was wearing a T-shirt that said GEEKS RULE.

"Hey, Cooper!" Ben said. "Happy birthday."

"It's great to see you guys," Cooper said, smiling. "Come on inside."

They followed Cooper inside to the living room. Clear plastic covered the flowery couch and loveseat.

"So where is everybody?" Ben asked.

"You're here!" Cooper replied cheerfully. "Let's get this party started!"

"Oh, great," Kevin moaned. "You mean nobody else is coming?"

"Well, I invited my grandma, but it's Bingo night," Cooper explained. "We don't need anybody else, anyway. This is going to be an awesome party. My mom even ordered a pizza."

Cooper motioned to a pizza box on the coffee table. Kevin flipped open the lid.

"There's only one slice in there," he said.

Cooper blushed. "Well, I might have eaten some of it while I was waiting for you guys. You're late."

Ben thrust a present into Cooper's hands. "Here, we got you something."

"Hey, cool!" he said, tearing off the paper. "A Captain Outrageous action figure! Just what I wanted!"

"We know," Gwen said dryly, "you told us."

Cooper raced out of the living room. Ben looked at the others and shrugged. They followed him down the hallway into Cooper's bedroom.

Shelves lined three walls of Cooper's room from corner to corner. The shelves were filled with what looked like every action figure ever made. The fourth wall contained Cooper's amazing computer setup. He had three monitors and five blinking hard drives.

Kevin pointed to a Captain Outrageous action figure sitting on top of one of the drives.

"Hey, you already have that," he said.

"I had *one,*" Cooper corrected him. "Everyone

knows you need two of each action figure. One to keep in the box, and one to take out and play with."

"That's it, I'm outta here," Kevin said. "I'm too old to play with action figures."

Cooper ran to the door and blocked it with his body. "Don't go! Forget about Captain Outrageous. Check out this wicked alien tech I just scored."

That was enough to stop Kevin. Trading in alien technology was a hobby of his, and one that had gotten him into trouble more than once. But Kevin was fascinated by each new device he came across. Each one was more surprising than the next.

Cooper sat at his desk and started typing into his keyboard. A starry scene popped up on the largest computer screen. Cooper zoomed in on a picture of two planets, a small brown one and a larger white one.

"I hacked into this intergalactic role-playing game," Cooper said. "It's way better than any game on Earth. I haven't been able to translate the alien writing, but I pretty much got it figured out. You pick a planet, and then use its weapons system to attack other planets. I'm the small brown planet.

I call it 'Planet Cooper.' I launched a totally sick attack on that white planet there, Planet Kevin."

"Hey!" Kevin protested.

"It's just a game," Cooper said. "I don't know the real name, but I call it 'Galaxy Wars.' You should try it."

Cooper started typing on the keyboard, and a weapons schematic appeared on the screen. The diagram was labeled with alien writing.

"That looks familiar," Kevin said thoughtfully.

"Yeah, whatever," Cooper said. His eyes glazed over as he played the game.

"Uh, Cooper, could we do something else?" Ben asked.

"Sure," Cooper said. He handed Ben a remote. "Why don't you turn on that TV over there?"

Ben sighed and switched on the television set. He pushed some clothes off of Cooper's bed and sat down. "Might as well make ourselves comfortable," he said.

The face of a newscaster appeared on the TV screen. She was holding a microphone and standing in front of Bellwood Town Hall. Behind her, people were running and screaming.

"Uh-oh," Gwen said. "This doesn't look good."

"Downtown Bellwood is under attack from an alien creature in a spaceship!" the newscaster announced. "Could this be one of the many forms of that menace, Ben Tennyson?"

Ben jumped up. "Sorry, Coop," he said. "Gotta run!"

CHAPTER TWO

Ben raced through the back streets of Bellwood, taking a shortcut downtown. His green souped-up muscle car was loaded with alien tech—and a killer engine.

"It's so unfair that the media keeps blaming everything on you," Julie said from the passenger seat. "You're the one saving everybody when aliens attack."

Kevin stuck his head between them. "It's not like he does it alone," he said. "Gwen and I have saved his butt more than once, you know."

"That's true," Julie agreed. "But at least you guys haven't been labeled Public Enemy Number One."

"It's not so bad," Ben said. Then he turned a corner, driving right into a crowd of protesters carrying signs.

"Keep Aliens Out of Bellwood!"

"Send Ben Back to Outer Space!"

"Ban Ben!"

"Okay, maybe it is," Ben admitted.

Ben steered the car to the curb and made his way through the crowd, followed by Kevin, Gwen, and Julie. Nobody even noticed Ben in his human form. All eyes were on the spaceship that was busy decimating downtown.

The donut-shaped ship wasn't much bigger than an SUV. A clear domed bubble rose up from the center of the donut. Ben could see the pilot, an alien with a furry-face and a twitching black nose. He looked panicked, and he seemed to have lost control of his ship. It dove low over the heads of the crowd, then picked up again and flew right through a billboard advertising Crystal Cola.

"Is that a spaceship, or a car from an amusement park ride?" Kevin asked.

"I don't know, but whatever it is, it's not from around here," Ben replied.

The ship veered up sharply, flying over the trees that lined the once-peaceful street. Leaves went flying in all directions as the alien ship sheared them right off.

A frightened man ran past them. "Somebody stop Ben Tennyson before he destroys us all!"

Ben sighed. "Really? Do they think I'm that lame?"

He held up his list and activated an alien form on the Ultrimatrix.

"Let's go Diamondhead!" Ben cried. He punched a button on the Ultrimatrix, and a bright green light washed over his body. When the light faded, an alien stood in Ben's place. Diamondhead's powerful body was made of a substance harder than diamond. Sharp crystalline points grew from his back, and he wore a sleeveless one-piece outfit that was black on the right side, and white on the left side. His hard-muscled upper arms looked like boulders, and his hands were hard-hitting hammers.

"I'll stabilize him for you," Gwen offered. Her grandmother was an Anodite alien, and Gwen had inherited several unique abilities from her. She raised both hands in the air, palms out, and waves of pink energy poured out from them. The pink energy formed a bubble around the ship just as it ricocheted off of a two-story office building, sending bricks and debris tumbling down below.

Gwen strained to hold the ship inside the bubble. She slowly lowered her hands, and the spaceship hovered a few feet above the street.

"My turn," Diamondhead said in a deep voice. The bubble evaporated, and Diamondhead's massive fist came crashing down on the front of the ship. The metal dented, but it didn't cripple the ship like Diamondhead had hoped. Whatever that metal was, it was tough stuff.

Inside, the alien pilot looked terrified. With a loud cry, Diamondhead picked up the ship and pounded it on the street. The pavement cracked, but the spaceship remained unharmed.

Frustrated now, Diamondhead raised both arms in the air.

BAM! He brought them both down on the clear hood covering the pilot, shattering it. The pilot covered his head with his hands.

"Please, please, don't hurt me!" the alien begged.

Kevin ran up and grabbed the controls from the pilot. He pulled some levers and pressed some buttons, and the ship lost power. Diamondhead pulled the alien out of his seat. He was about the size of a five-year-old Earth child.

"What brings you to Bellwood?" Diamondhead asked.

"I come in peace!" the alien yelled. "I am not here to attack. I am looking for someone called Ben Tennyson. My planet needs his help!"

Diamondhead set the alien on the ground. Green light flashed over his body, and Ben returned to his human form.

"You know, I really should start giving out my cell phone number," Ben said. "Things would be so much easier!"

GEAR UP! IT'S HERO TIME!

Get ready for action with the Omnitrix X10

Works with collectible mini figures!
(sold separately)

Secret code

Secret code appears!

Connect Online!
Play exclusive games on
www.bandai.com/Ben10

In Stores Now!